ORGANIZATIONAL SKILLS

Maximize Success Academy

We believe you are successful at present, but we facilitate, mentor, and provide strategies to maximize your success and bring out the genius in you. (Mind Over Logic To Bring The Genius In You)

Dean Mukesh

Edhas Group Inc.
ONTARIO, CANADA.
https://maximizesuccessacademy.com
http://deanmukesh.com

DISCLAIMER

NOTE TO READERS:

This publication contains the opinions and ideas of its author. We intend to provide helpful and informative material on the subjects addressed. The strategies outlined in this book do not guarantee to make any particular result

. It may not suit every individual. The reader needs to know that the publisher or the author does not provide financial, legal, or professional service or advice. The reader is advised to contact an expert before drawing any inference or taking a suggestion from the book.

No warranty is made for the accuracy or completeness of this book's information or references. This is a disclaimer of the publisher and the author for any responsibility for the loss, liability, or risk of any kind, personal or otherwise, which may arise as an effect of using the book's contents, whether directly or indirectly.

Dedication

This book is dedicated to Raman for his Outstanding Organizational Skills as I saw him leading his company to new heights as Vice President I learned few strategies from him. Thanks, Raman. I am proud of you.

About The Author

Dean Mukesh is a job strategist, success facilitator and productivity mentor. He believes you are already successful in life and he helps you, guides you, mentors you, coaches you, and provides you strategies to maximize your success. He is a dynamic and passionate person who understands that knowledge increases by sharing with others. He believes it brings a positive change to one's life, helping individuals shape their thoughts and goals into dreams, becoming their reality at later stages of life. He has been following his adventurous path in Canada for over 35 years. His exclusive and unique traits encourage him to evoke the same burning desire in others – to live life to the fullest and promote growth, wisdom, love, happiness, success, and deeper fulfilment. He understands that people worldwide face various challenges in life in fears, doubts, anxiety and traumas. He also senses that to motivate, encourage, support and help people believe and achieve the most out of life, and from whatever it is that's holding them back, a strong inspiration is required. He then stepped forward to explore and encourage himself to learn theta-healing techniques to get truly connected to the power of the Creator. He affirms that living in this society. His moral duty is to share his knowledge and wisdom with others to educate themselves comfortably at home at a low cost. His objective for teaching these techniques is to positively impact an individual's life by motivating them with nature's powers.

INTRODUCTION

After finishing this book, you will be saying "WOW," because I will give you some great success tips. In fact, in this book, you will find several free pieces of information to help maximize and speed up the growth of your life. So, as I like to say, "Be successful, surround yourself with those who are successful."

maximizesuccessacademy.com

PRÉFACE

Dear readers, this book speaks to my self-journey working in an enterprise environment and has seen numerous challenges during my early working years. At that point, one of my mentors guided me to start attending courses, seminars and workshops. Therefore, I compiled these real-life scenarios of what an individual faces in dealing with complex clients. These real case studies will assist you in creating an association along with your life. In this way, you'll get inspiration for supplanting all your negative considerations with positive mentality affirmations. I moreover reported the negative convictions to let go and the positive change of mindset affirmation to divert focus. This made a difference in my life, and I believe that you will feel that after going through this book. I empower you to grant me your feedback as well.

Dean Mukesh.

Contents

INTRODUCTION 20

Techniques of Removing Clutter 24

Outline the Priorities 32

Scheduling your Time 40

Keeping an Efficient To-Do List.................... 48

Operating a Paper or Paperless Storage System 56

How to be organized at work?...................... 64

Organizing Your Inbox 72

Organizing Your Mails.................................... 80

Avoid the Causes of Disorganizing 89

Importance of Discipline................................ 97

CHAPTER ONE
INTRODUCTION

Welcome to the brainstorming on Organizational Skills. Good organizational abilities can help you in a variety of situations, including personal and professional ones. Organization can boost a person's overall productivity and project management while also affecting his memory and retention. These abilities do not come naturally; they require a lot of hard work and practice. However, anyone can learn to quit looking for lost items and become more organized with coaching and the correct tools.

A person must first study effective training techniques and recommendations to help him attain his objective to learn superior organizing skills effectively. With this assistance, everyone may look at their existing routines and devise a new strategy for becoming more organized in their lives.

At the end of the book, you will be able to understand the following:
- Techniques of Removing Clutter
- Outline the Priorities
- Scheduling your Time
- Keeping an Efficient To-Do List

- Operating a Paper or Paperless Storage System
- How to be organized at work?
- Organizing Your Inbox
- Organizing Your Mails
- Avoid the Causes of Disorganizing
- Importance of Discipline

By completing this book, you will have a better understanding of negative beliefs you may have, and you may go through and form even new change of positive mindset affirmations which you may wish to have as part of your life.

Let's begin the journey…

CHAPTER TWO
Techniques of Removing Clutter

Removing clutter saves you a lot of time looking for essential things, cleaning your space and focusing on tasks.

Let's take a look at the situation of Sara.

Sara decided she would spend her Saturday afternoon clearing out the clutter present in the family den. She thought its the best time to clear it off. She sorted all items into three boxes and labelled them as to keep, throw and donate. She decided to throw broken toys and old paper things away.

But then Sara used to find those things here and there on her way. She decided to keep everything but then realized it is difficult to stock up everything at her place.

By the end of the afternoon, Sara had managed to fill the donation box and throw it away. Then, she was left with just the things she wanted to keep at their place and never had trouble organizing.

Executive Summary

Having so much clutter in your workplace and home distracts you from focusing on tasks, and it is essential to get rid of clutter to work in a pleasant and vibrant atmosphere.

Negative Beliefs You May Have

- I am not able to focus on tasks
- I am not able to sort things
- I am not able to get rid of clutter at the workplace

Positive Change of Mindset Affirmations You May Wish To Have

- I can sort out things at the workplace
- I can focus on my work after clearing the place
- Now I am working in a vibrant atmosphere

- Now I am organized, and it is easy for me to find things at work
- I can utilize my time properly after having the clean space

You may write your affirmations below:

For example, "You must be plain and simple at the workplace."

- DEAN MUKESH

CHAPTER THREE
Outline the Priorities

Prioritizing works in professional and personal life helps us in utilizing time effectively. In addition, it builds your confidence by finishing tasks on time.

Let's take a look at the situation of John:

John wants to become more organized and realized he has some free time to do it. However, when he looked around at what needed to be done, he began to feel overwhelmed and discouraged. But he sat down and wrote a list of things to be achieved. After preparing the list, he prioritized the tasks on his lists.

Still feeling swamped, John went over the list again and divided different projects based on priority. Finally, he marked which tasks he wanted to take care of first and then later. Now that John had lined out what he wanted to do and in what order, he was ready to tackle his list of jobs and get organized.

Executive Summary

Listing important works and prioritizing which tasks are to be completed first gives you the complete knowledge of finishing that task. Having self-awareness helps you to improve your performance while performing tasks.

Negative Beliefs You May Have

- I don't have self-awareness
- I am not able to prioritize my work
- I am not able to list my jobs at the workplace

Positive Change of Mindset Affirmations You May Wish To Have

- I can list all the tasks at work.
- I can prioritize my assignments at the workplace.
- I am utilizing my time correctly to complete my work.

- I am creating a schedule to complete my tasks.
- Now I know how to plan incomplete tasks.

You may write your affirmations below:

> "You must schedule your priorities to achieve success in your life."
>
> – DEAN MUKESH

CHAPTER FOUR
Scheduling your Time

Preparing a schedule is vital in the success or growth of any company. It helps in balancing the work and planning the activities to be carried out in a company.

Let's look at the following situation of Kiara:

Kiara has a critical report due at the end of the week and is having trouble finishing it on schedule. Even though she wrote it on her master calendar and gave herself several reminders, she feels she lacks enough focus to concentrate on the project. So, one night, Kiara decided to work on the task at home, turned off her cell phone, and went into her room to be alone and work on her report.

She noticed she worked much better without the everyday distractions she was letting get in her way. She finished her report two days early and was very excited about her progress. But when she tried to print her final copy, her home printer broke. Kiara panicked at first and wasn't sure what to do. But she remembered that she could print it at the local library instead. Once she had her final, published report in hand, she was grateful that she had left herself enough time for possible mistakes and was able to save her report in time.

Executive Summary

Listing the vital work and scheduling those tasks at the right time helps in meeting the deadlines. In addition, having a proper schedule gives clarity for the employees to finish the assignments on time.

Negative Beliefs You May Have

- I am not able to plan well
- I am not able to schedule important activities
- I don't have clarity in completing tasks

Positive Change of Mindset Affirmations You May Wish To Have

- I can plan essential tasks at work.
- Now I know how to schedule activities at the workplace
- Now I know how to be organized and simple
- I can implement my plan when performing tasks
- I can progress at work

You may write your affirmations below:

> "Make an effort to complete as many tasks as you can at your workplace."
>
> - DEAN MUKESH

CHAPTER FIVE

Keeping an Efficient To-Do List

A To-do list is essential to carry out all activities at the workplace. Accomplishing the tasks on to-do lists helps you in reaching your targets on time.

Let's look at the following situation of Dave:

Dave is reviewing his schedule lately and realized he had missed several necessary appointments and meetings while also not accomplishing anything on his to-do list. He then planned what activities are to be completed to help improve his productivity and memory skills. He bought a calendar to plan his activities.

He checked his schedule for the other weeks and made notes. Next, he made a list of projects he had recently started and didn't complete for so long and would not linger on his list any longer. Finally, when he made a list for his home, he marked three things that needed to be done urgently. Dave then scored the top four tasks that he could do right away and decided to tackle those first. Now that he had his assignments and projects organized, Dave felt like he had a better handle on his schedule and time.

Executive Summary

An efficient to-do list always gives you the motivation to finish your tasks on time. It is essential to have a to-do list while starting a project to be easy for employees to follow the flow of work.

Negative Beliefs You May Have

- I don't have a to-do list at the workplace
- I am not able to maintain a schedule and time
- I am not able to accomplish my to-do list

Positive Change of Mindset Affirmations You May Wish To Have

- I can prepare an efficient to-do list
- I can accomplish tasks on a to-do list
- Now I can maintain schedule and time
- I can spend productive time following my to-do lists
- Now I know how to provide constructive solutions at the workplace

You may write your affirmations below:

> "Confidence boosts you to complete tasks on time at the workplace."
>
> - DEAN MUKESH

CHAPTER SIX

Operating a Paper or Paperless Storage System

An organization must have all the records in a paper or paperless storage system. In addition, they must have access to the storage whenever it is required.

Let's look at the following situation of Rosy:

Rosy is going through her office and wanted to organize her mounds of paperwork. But then, she realized she needed a better way to store everything she needed to keep. So first, she decided to scan and copy several of her document files to the computer to save the storage area. But her particular documents, such as various manuals (employee, policy and procedure, etc.), she thought she would have kept that physical document for future reference.

So she developed a file system for her paper storage and her paperless storage that worked best for her everyday use, including files and folders that held her work deadlines. Lastly, she set aside a particular folder for her older and less essential documents to archive.

She put them in the back of the filing cabinet's bottom drawer, which does not disturb her from doing work.

Executive Summary

The company must have access to the records of its activities. It helps them to reach out to the documents or files on time. They can have access to their papers on everyday basics.

Negative Beliefs You May Have

- I don't have the records of previous work.
- I don't have access to the storage of the company
- I am not able to track daily activities at work

Positive Change of Mindset Affirmations You May Wish to Have:

- I can track all the activities of the company
- I have access to the storage of the company
- I can review my old records quickly when required
- Now I can organize my work by storing them
- I am making necessary changes to the files and documents easily.

You may write your affirmations below:

"Always make sure everything is in the proper place at work."

- DEAN MUKESH

CHAPTER SEVEN

How to be organized at work?

While working on a project, it is essential to reorganize to work better and complete the project on time. In addition, organizing at work simplifies your tasks at the workplace.

Let's look at the scenario of Arya:

Arya was assigned to work on a company slideshow presentation for the next week in his office. After coming to work, he realized he needs to help him perform better and complete the project on time. So first, he removed all of his other projects off of his desk since he would not need to work on them for the next week or so. He then checked his desk drawers and file cabinet for files to quickly access them all the time.

Finally, he sorted the place and rearranged everything he would need to be in arm's reach so he wouldn't have to get back up to find something. Now that everything was arranged to Arya's office space was organized to his workflow, he knew he could complete the project without any problems.

Executive Summary

While working on a new project, it is essential to organize your place by removing things related to the previous projects. Also, it is important to keeps the supplies necessary for the project and can be readily accessed.

Negative Beliefs You May Have

- I don't know how to organize at work.
- I don't have the required items necessary for the project
- I am not having access to all the supplies at work

Positive Change of Mindset Affirmations You May Wish To Have

- I can place all the stores in handy whenever required
- I can organize my workplace properly

- I can arrange everything on my desk to use when required.
- Now I know how to finish my tasks on time.
- Now I can spend time wisely by organizing my work.

You may write your affirmations below:

"You get happiness when you complete tasks with your hard and smart work."

- DEAN MUKESH

CHAPTER EIGHT

Organizing Your Inbox

Organizing is easy by dividing the work into simple tasks. After working for some time, you will be able to notice a significant change in the workplace.

Let's look at the following scenario of Aadya:

Aadya has decided to use her day off to clean out her messy attic and hopefully reorganize the storage items she has in there. She left her cell phone downstairs and made a shortlist of everything that would need to be done in there for it to be finished. She groaned when she realized she would need to sweep and dust the entire area to help clean out all of the dirt. Aadya decided she would do this task first so she could go ahead and get it over with.

When she finished, she divided the rest of the work into smaller, quicker tasks, such as removing boxes and cleaning out trash items. After she had worked for a few hours and had completed several studies on her list, she took a short break and got a snack. When she came back, she felt more energized to finish the entire attic by the end of the day.

Executive Summary

While working in the workplace, it is essential to have a vibrant atmosphere. It boosts your confidence at the workplace and helps you in completing tasks on time.

Negative Beliefs You May Have

- I don't know how to divide work into simple tasks
- I am not able to finish tasks on time
- I am not able to clean my workplace

FILE STORAGE

Folder structure

☐ Project name
   ☐ Emails
   ☐ Attachments
   ☐ Documents
   ☐ Spreadsheets

Naming convention

Date YY.MM.DD
Project name
Name / why kept for ref

Positive Change of Mindset Affirmations You May Wish to Have

- I am energetic in doing tasks at work
- I can finish my assignments on time
- I am punctual while doing tasks
- Now I can divide my work and complete it on time
- Now I can clean my workplace

You may write your affirmations below:

File storage.

"Start working on improving your habits to make impossible tasks possible."

- DEAN MUKESH

CHAPTER NINE

Organizing Your Mails

A company must always make sure to delete junk files and keep important ones in storage. It helps them to find the essential files when required.

Let's look at the following scenario of Gauri:

Gauri sat down at her desk and opened her email. She was amazed at how many messages she had at once, many of them about upcoming deadlines and correspondence from her boss. She decided she better sort through it and got it organized before she missed anything important. First, she created several folders and subfolders by order of importance that she could use to sort her messages.

She deleted several emails that were no longer needed or did not pertain to her. Then, with her remaining emails, Gauri sorted them into the appropriate email folder, including "Emails from the

Boss," "Upcoming Meetings," and "Projects."

After her inbox was almost transparent, Gauri set up several new delivery rules that would help her keep track of her emails, including highlighting meeting reminders in green and flagging all assignments and projects with a red flag. In addition, any emails from unknown addresses were set up to go into her Spam folder. When she was finished, Gauri could finally find and read emails that needed her attention instead of seeing them among the mass amount of messages.

Executive Summary

It is vital to clear unnecessary mails and sort all emails accordingly. Highlighting can be done where ever required. Sorting messages from the boss, project and other news are essential.

Negative Beliefs You May Have

- I don't know how to sort my mails
- I don't know how to manage my inbox
- I am not able to delete unimportant messages

Positive Change of Mindset Affirmations You May Wish To Have

- I can arrange my emails in the inbox properly.
- I can sort the correspondences on their priority at work

- I know how to highlight my remainders
- I can respond to people after sorting mails
- Now it is easy to look for essential emails after sorting.

INBOX FOLDERS.
☐ FROM VIP.
☐ TO ACTION
☐ TO FOLLOW UP.
☐ FILING

CATEGORIES
MEETING — ORANGE.
DEADLINE — RED
IN CALENDAR — GREEN

DELIVERY RULES
QUICK CLICKS ? INSTEAD OF DELIVERY RULES
END OF DAY RULES?
FRIDAY RULES ?

You may write your affirmations below:

"Plan your time properly and utilize it to complete your high priority tasks to achieve success in your life."
- DEAN MUKESH

CHAPTER TEN

Avoid the Causes of Disorganizing

Trying to keep everything at the workplace doesn't create a vibrant atmosphere. It is essential to get rid of stuff that is no longer important.

Let's look at the following scenario of Ruby:

Ruby decided to see her friend, Charles, at his office. When she walked inside, she was amazed at the mess his office was in and how disorganized everything was. She asked how his office got this way, and he exclaimed that there wasn't a problem with it.

"You are so disorganized! I bet you don't get rid of anything and try to keep everything!" Ruby said.

"Only the things I think I'll need later." He answered. "Besides, I started a new organization routine, but I haven't been able to do it every day."

Ruby explained how keeping everything and not sticking with a routine can cause further disorganization. Then, she offered to help him develop a plan to kick the bad habits and create newer, better patterns to get organized.

"Once you form better, more helpful habits, you'll be more organized in no time!" Ruby said.

Executive Summary

Disorganizing at work always lands you in trouble when you need to find anything significant. However, sticking to healthy habits will develop you as a person and helps you to become more organized.

Negative Beliefs You May Have

- I don't know how to be organized
- I am not able to develop healthy habits at work
- I am not able to stick to a routine

Positive Change of Mindset Affirmations You May Wish To Have

- I can stick to a proper routine at the workplace
- Now I am more organized at work
- I can develop healthy habits at the workplace
- I can plan well and complete things on time
- Now I know how to be active and respond quickly at the workplace.

You may write your affirmations below:

> "Organizing keeps you grounded and helps you in developing healthy habits."
>
> - DEAN MUKESH

CHAPTER ELEVEN

Importance of Discipline

Organizing your workplace will keep you relaxed and let you finish your tasks on time with ease. In addition, it boosts your mood to work correctly.

Let's look at the following scenario of Josh:

"I finally did it!" exclaimed Josh.

Josh had finally organized his office in preparation for starting on a new client account in a few weeks. He knew he would need a clean and organized office to work in, so he realized he needed to take care of it sooner rather than later. Once it was ready, he made a daily and weekly to-do list that he must keep organized, such as arranging his desk area and putting away any tools or supplies he used. After that, he decided to stay with his current systems for several weeks or several meetings or projects and then see how they worked in his favour. Then he would see if anything needed to be changed or altered.

As he finished, Josh got a call from his friend, Charlie, asking if he requires help to paint his garbage.

"No thanks," Josh said. "I've got to get my office and myself in order if I'm going to be ready to take on this account on time!"

Executive Summary

Organizing is compulsory when you are working in a professional or personal space. It helps you to arrange your things properly and make it easy to find them when required.

Negative Beliefs You May Have:

- I do not know how to keep my place organized
- I am not able to arrange my things
- I always look for things when I need something important

Positive Change of Mindset Affirmations You May Wish To Have

- I can organize my place and arrange everything properly.
- Now I know how organizing helps me in doing better work.

- Now I know the importance of collecting things on time.
- Organizing my space helped me in developing good habits.
- Now I am sticking to the proper routine at work.

You may write your affirmations below:

"You have the power to do or not to do, and your decision defines your destiny."

- DEAN MUKESH

If You Have Got Any Affirmation, Questions Or Recommendations Like To Grant A Feedback.

It Will Be Ideal If You Visit The Following Link

Deanmukesh.Com/Aqs

For Productivity Mentorship
AND
To Facilitate Your Prosperity
AND
To Become a high-flying CEO or Executive book 1 to 1 session with Dean Mukesh.
Visit deanmukesh.com/1to1

- Coming Soon
- Sign up to get early notification for audio-video meditation and get an audio-video change of mindset affirmations with the book at no cost.
Go to
deanmukesh.com/mindset.

TO HAVE MAXIMIZE SUCCESS IN YOUR LIFE

MEET US!!

deanmukesh.com/meetus

Printed in Great Britain
by Amazon